First published by Parragon in 2012

Parragon
Chartist House
15-17 Trim Street
Bath BA1 1HA, UK
www.parragon.com

ISBN 978-1-4454-8367-2

Printed in China

Goodnight
Little One

PaRRagon

Bath·New York·Singapore·Hong Kong·Cologne·Delhi
Tübbaume·Amsterdam·Johannesburg·Shenzhen

Little donkey on the hill,
        Standing there so very still.

Making faces at the skies,

Little donkey
close your eyes.

Little monkey in the tree,
Swinging there so merrily.
Throwing coconuts at the skies,

Little monkey
close *your* eyes.

Silly sheep that slowly crop,
Night has come and you must stop.

Chewing grass beneath the skies,
Silly sheep now close *your* eyes.

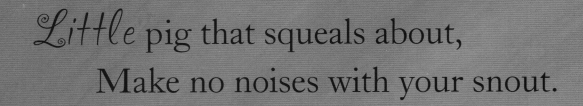

Little pig that squeals about,
Make no noises with your snout.

No more squealing to the skies,

Little pig now
        close *your* eyes.

Wild young birds that sweetly sing,
Curve your heads beneath your wing.
Dark night covers all the skies,
Wild young birds now close *your* eyes.

Old black cat down in the barn,
Keeping five small kittens warm.
Let the wind blow in the skies,

Dear old black cat
close *your* eyes.

Little child all tucked in bed,
Looking such a sleepy head.
Stars are quiet in the skies,

Little child now
close *your* eyes.